Could Have Been Verse

David Winship

WARNING!
May contain traces of serious writing.

The Missing Moon

Midnight, in the middle of June.
I hope sleep arrives very soon,
But the sky's very clear
And I must say I fear
That someone has stolen the moon!

We're not due a lunar eclipse.
Has Nature played one of her tricks?
I'm suspicious, in truth,
Of the cat on the roof,
Who's sitting there licking its lips.

Social Media and the Fruit Fly

Information and communication technology has transformed our lives over the past few decades and a key development has been the emergence of social media. The immediacy of communication has fundamentally altered our time perception. This should be really good news for species that only have short life cycles, like the fruit fly.

The fruit fly is a busy thing,
She doesn't have much time.
She has to do her whole life's work
Before it's half past nine!

Drosophila is her real name,
And that is just so wrong -
She can never introduce herself,
For it would take too long!

She'd really love to stop and chat -
The chance just never comes.
There's only time to multiply -
She has to do her sums!

Social media is the answer,
And she can take her pick -
Use Facebook, Twitter or LinkedIn
To say stuff really quick.

Although she'll never know her kids
(They'll barely get to meet),

She'll tell them her life story
In just a single tweet!

She'll tell them stuff like where and how
To fly and eat and drink.
Their whole life is ahead of them -
That's shorter than you think!

The Time Travel Paradox

You might think you can't make things unhappen (i.e. you can make an omelette out of an egg but you can't make an egg out of an omelette), but what if you could? There's a time travel paradox - the danger that someone could go back in time and change the course of history, e.g. by killing their grandfathers before they're born. Given the opportunity, I think all time travellers would in fact change stuff. It could be that they're here among us now and they're itching to change the course of history. We've got to stop them! Basically, we need to make sure they don't do anything! My proposal is to get everyone to do absolutely nothing until such time as we can identify the pesky time-travellers and get this sorted out!

I intend to go into politics on a global level, advocating lethargic solutions, incentivising idle people who are inclined not to make anything of their lives. I think it's imperative that we save our future by doing absolutely nothing for as long as it takes to resolve the situation. I intend to set a good example by having a nice lie-down right now, and I suggest you do the same! Save our future - do nothing!

If time travel actually happens,
Then everything really unravels.
I won't write no more,
You've heard it before -
I wrote it next week on my travels.

Are you a head, heart or hands person? Everyone, it seems, is ruled by one of these, or a combination of them. For a limited period, I'm going to be ruled by my left knee, because, hey, the head, heart and hands have been monopolising things for long enough.

To Boldly Go

Astronauts wishing to join NASA's space-flying corps have to submit to a gruelling application process - probing interviews and evaluations to discover which candidates have what the writer Tom Wolfe referred to as the 'right stuff'. Once selected, they undergo a rigorous two-year training program.

I'd love to be an astronaut,
Although the training's tough.
I don't mind floating weightlessly,
I'll do the maths and stuff.

I'll study the Russian language
And meteorology;
I'll dive into tanks of water
And learn astronomy.

And then when I'm trained and ready,
I'll wave to all you guys
Before my NASA rocket ship
Propels me to the skies.

I'll aim for a lunar crater
Or maybe fly to Mars
Or sail off past Andromeda
And head for distant stars.

There's just one thing can stop me now,
Before I say goodbye -
A minor little phobia:
I'm much too scared to fly!

Basil

He's a great connoisseur of culinary arts,
So very discerning 'bout puff pastry tarts,
Also pastries and pies and cookies and cakes -
Oh yes, Basil's around when anyone bakes!

He'll state his opinions and offer advice
And try new concoctions without thinking twice.
I'm sure he'll soon start his own cookery blog -
But it might surprise you... this foodie's a dog!

*Most puppies outgrow their natural impulse to
put everything in their mouths. Not my son's dog,
Basil! This cockapoo eats everything from photo
albums to underwear! And if anyone does any
baking.... well, it's just carnage!*

If penguins were judged by their ability to climb trees, they would go through their lives believing they were useless. That's not right. From now on, I'm going to judge *everyone* by their ability to climb trees. It's only fair to the penguins.

Something I Wanted To Tell You

There's something I wanted to tell you,
But I cannot think what it was.
It flew out my brain
Like a rat down a drain.
If it comes back I'll keep it indoors.

It's bound to turn up somewhere
In Tilehurst or Timbuctoo.
It can't drive a car,
So it can't have gone far.
Perhaps it went looking for you?

To Bee or not to Bee

Bees pollinate over 80% of all flowering plants, including 70 of the top 100 human food crops. Over 270 species of bee have been recorded in Britain alone. Not all bees are social, but honey bees lead complex lives, where development and survival are dependent on social interaction. It is believed that William Shakespeare was a beekeeper.

Some bees make nests in hollow trees,
Some just live in hives,
Some burrow deep down under ground,
And stay there all their lives.

They're sophisticated creatures,
It's hard to understand
The way they just cooperate,
The way they lend a hand.

I never did identify
The one that went for me.
It neither was a burrower
Nor a lender bee!

Minnows in a Stream

My love is like a motorboat
All badly choked with rust.
My love is like a field of wheat
That's turned to clouds of dust.

It doesn't matter how I sleep,
I'll never catch the dream,
And love was just a fleeting light,
A minnow in a stream.

My love has left me flound'ring
In the wake of broken trust.
My love's become malignant now,
It poisons all I touch.

I know that ev'ry sleep might bring
Another chance to dream,
But hopes of love just scatter round
Like minnows in a stream.

From time to time I think I see
A flash, a glint, a gleam,
But hopes of love dart from my hands
Like minnows in a stream.

Politics

Politics is just too confusing.
I go with one party, then switch.
I go right and then left, and then vice versa,
And I don't even know which is which!

Carrie's Magic Flask of Tea

One day my luck just disappeared
And life became all wild and weird.
Way past the point of no return,
I didn't know which way to turn.
The thing that served to rescue me
Was Carrie's magic flask of tea.

So word got round and doctors swore
This liquid gold could be a cure
For common colds and leprosy,
Mad cow disease and dysentery.
Now all you need for Housemaid's Knee
Is Carrie's magic flask of tea.

The flags of peace were soon unfurled
And love broke out around the world.
They sang and danced in South Sudan,
Iraq and Greece and Kazakhstan.
The thing that set these people free

Was Carrie's magic flask of tea.

The CIA and KGB
Tried hard to get the recipe.
They sent their spies to Golders Green
And every tea shop in between.
But no one solved the mystery
Of Carrie's magic flask of tea.

When I'm old and the end is nigh
And I see angels flying high,
I won't need cash or mobile phone;
My credit card can stay at home.
The only thing I'll take with me
Is Carrie's magic flask of tea.

The Swallow

Here is
whiteness
a token of blue
flat as a plate
deep as a slice of the ocean

Turning
shimmering plate
yawning flat
as daylight starts to taper

Breathing low
waking ripples glide

An asterisk of wings
high and blue-pointed
stretching wide a tiny throat
perhaps a scatter of silver notes
to free the ears from the past

The colours will return
though the songs are dying
fast

A soft flurry of wings
and gone

The polar ice caps may be in danger of melting and causing the oceans to rise. Save the Arctic. Donate ice.

Andromeda

You haven't got time for a snooze,
I'm afraid I've got some bad news.
Get ready, hold onto your hats,
Go gather your dogs and your cats!

Some people will panic, it's true -
We'll keep it between me and you:
Andromeda's about to collide -
We cannot escape if we tried!

It could be goodbye, au revoir,
So light up a big fat cigar!
And I think we might have the time
To open a bottle of wine.

The experts are now all agreed,
It's coming towards us at speed.
Though it's getting closer each hour,
We don't have to lie down and cower.

No, let's act before it arrives,
Let's do stuff to help us survive.
I'll go out and get a tin hat
I don't want my head to go splat.

We must be resourceful and shrewd -
We'll stock up on water and food.
And when it's about to collide,
Get under a table and hide!

How long have we got, you may ask,

To do all these onerous tasks?
I cannot allay all your fears....
We've only got four billion years!!

Snoring

Her snoring is phenomenal.
It's off the Richter Scale.
The buildings shake for miles around
And people quake and quail.

When the moon begins to wobble,
It comes as no surprise
That huge waves roll down rivers
And birds fall from the skies.

The sound is like a fighter jet
Complete with sonic boom,
But if you dare to mention it,
She flounces from the room.

Our leaders must take action now.

We're doing what we can,
But she MUST be stopped from sleeping -
We need a blanket ban!

That'll be Me

When the grim reaper has caught up with me
Please scatter my ashes upon a calm sea.

When the gulls, fishing for crabs, have all flown
And when they stop fighting and soar off alone,
That'll be me.
When the waves gather and curl and unfurl
And when they give up and dissolve into foam,
That'll be me.

Don't lay me in wood, all lacquered to last.
I don't want fine lace or handles of brass.
When I'm adrift and don't answer my name,
Let all the sea birds and fish lay their claim.
When all the laughter has drained out of me
Please scatter my ashes upon a calm sea.

Then when you're taking a stroll in the sand
And breezes send whispers from ocean to land,
That'll be me.
You may hear lapping of waves on the shore;
You may feel spray on your face and your hands:
That'll be me.

Beans on Toast

I'm not exactly a resourceful cook. Left to my own devices in the kitchen, I'll invariably make my signature dish, beans on toast, pretty much every time. The most "gourmet" I get is when I add a little grated cheese. You can survive on beans on toast, right?

He ate nothing but beans and some toast.
"I can survive!" he would boast.
But to his disgust, he choked on the crust,
Killed by the beans and some toast!

Sand Creek

This poem refers to the 1864 Sand Creek Massacre, in which a contingent of Colorado militia slaughtered over 150 Arapaho and Cheyenne, mostly women and children, at a settlement in eastern Colorado. Believing the US soldiers would not fire upon anyone standing under the Stars and Stripes, Cheyenne leader Black Kettle mounted the flag above his tipi in the middle of the village. The poem is written from Black Kettle's perspective during the night before the atrocities.

In the year of 1864
In the moon of popping trees
On the banks of the Arkansas
When the water starts to freeze

The stars have gone out one by one
The moon's turned pale and weak
The spirits will not gaze upon
My children at Sand Creek

The Stars and Stripes are flying high
Above me as I sleep
In a dream I hear my children cry
Why is it that they weep?

The sky's been dark since war began
Please let us live in peace
I reach out for the white chief's hand
The killing now must cease

Is that death's wing that flashes past
All draped in silver light?
And do I hear a trumpet blast
For souls to start their flight?

The stars have gone out one by one
The moon's turned pale and weak
The spirits will not gaze upon
My children at Sand Creek

Tonight the lights are going out
For the children at Sand Creek.

We Shall Never Surrender

The National Service Act 1948 imposed conscription on all males aged between 18 and 41 who had to register for "National Service" long after the Second World War had ended. As my dad served in the army, I just assumed he was away fighting for our country.

I thought dad was the bravest man
The world had ever seen.
He crossed the sea to Germany
To fight for England's queen.

I thought he'd got the Charing Cross
During the long campaign;
I think I must have got it wrong -
It's where he caught his train.

Turns out he'd got his dates all wrong
And never found the war.
The Germans refused to fight him
In 1954!

My Doomy Gloomy Universe

I try to protect people from my bad days, but that doesn't mean I can protect myself from them. Robin Williams once said: "I think the saddest people always try their hardest to make people happy because they know what it's like to feel absolutely worthless and they don't want anyone else to feel like that."

Things are seldom what they seem,
Nice things disappear in steam.
You may think I'm just plain perverse
In my doomy gloomy universe,

Write some words, I'll twist them round
Until their meaning can't be found,
It's not a blessing, it's a curse,
This doomy gloomy universe.

If something's good I'll make it bad.
I'll turn the happy into sad
And if it's bad I'll make it worse
In my doomy gloomy universe.

I can't be cheered up any more;
All your jokes are threats of war.
You won't get through while I'm immersed
In my doomy gloomy universe.

Round here somewhere there's a key,
So please don't worry, I'll get free.
I'll put this nightmare in reverse -
Stupid doomy gloomy universe!

You know that look in someone's eyes when you're sitting at a table with them and they're totally mesmerised by your charm, wit and intelligence? Me neither.

The Headless Pigeon

A friend of mine told me she'd found a headless pigeon in her garden and couldn't understand how such a tragic event could have occurred. After examining it, she said that, apart from the missing head, everything else seemed just fine!

There was a young pigeon called Fred,
Who woke up and thought he was dead!
It gave him a scare,
He looked everywhere -
The fact is he'd just lost his head.

Had he lost it during a fight
With a mad and brutal red kite?
Perhaps a strong breeze
Or maybe a sneeze
Had blown it away in the night?

A head doesn't grow back with time.
You can't get a new one online.
But Fred didn't care
And flew in the air,
Since ev'rything else felt just fine!

Sardines in a Can

The London Tube system is a unique way to travel around the city, especially at the height of the rush hour - people squashed together like sardines in complete silence. Budget airlines offer the same sort of experience - they're even contemplating squeezing in more passengers by having them stand up!

If sardines in a can could ever get out,
They'd find it delightful, without any doubt.
They'd relax on some toast
For an hour at most,
And then they'd enjoy a nice wander about.

There's all kinds of things they might like to pursue:
A trip to the park or a day at the zoo?
But I'd give them advice -
Rush-hour tubes are not nice,
And avoid cheap airlines whatever you do!

The Olive Branch

With listing ship I search for land;
The sails look sad and torn.
The compass cannot offer me
Safe passage through the storm.

I'm tossed upon the sea of life
And all the charts are lost.
I send a dove to look for land
With all my fingers crossed.

An olive branch is all I ask,
Like Noah in the flood.
But on the deck are feathers strewn,
And a spot or two of blood.

The Martian

I think if you were abducted by aliens, the best strategy would be to wander around making very loud gargling noises until they conclude that you're not the intelligent life form described in their brochures. Then they'll probably just send you back with some kind of microchip in your head.

But why haven't we seen more evidence of extraterrestrial life? The Fermi paradox, named after physicist Enrico Fermi, is the apparent contradiction between the high probability estimates for the existence of extraterrestrial civilisations, on the one hand, and the total lack of evidence for this, on the other. If the universe is 13 billion years old and if there are billions of stars with planets around them that might have developed intelligent civilisations, then... where is everybody?

If a Martian should land here and capture me,
I would need a good plan, I think you'll agree.
Yes, I'd panic a bit, but then I'd regroup
And make a loud noise like I'm drowning in soup -
If he'd been expecting intelligent life,
He might just give up and go home to his wife.

It could be this planet is simply a zoo,
Where extraterrestrials watch me and you.
I expect they're laughing but maybe they're not,
I bet there's a queue and it costs quite a lot.

I think they'll decide that our progress is stuck
And they don't have the time for us to catch up.

I'm being quite rude here, I have to confess,
But I don't think E.T. will keep our address,
For he and his friends will be in no doubt -
Our behaviour suggests we'll wipe ourselves out.

But none of us know what future awaits…
The truth is I hope that we all become mates.

The M31 galaxy is moving towards the Milky Way at about 250,000 miles an hour. Cover your head and do not use an elevator.

Eric and the Christmas Orange

Sprawled on the Sunday Telegraph,
A blanket round his knees,
He coughed and waved and said 'Hey, Guv,
Pound for an orange, please?'

It startled me to hear his voice.
I'm sure you would agree -
An orange seemed the oddest choice.
Why not a cup of tea?

I don't know why I lingered there
As buses came and went.
I heard a tale so sweet and rare
Inside his makeshift tent.

Eric told me of one winter time
When he'd been left alone -
Kids gathered round a Christmas pine
Inside the children's home.

An orange hung from every tip,
One fruit for every child;
While all around him licked their lips,
He watched in awe and smiled.

Four years old and just arrived,
He had no friends as such;
He stood amongst them, mesmerised,
But didn't dare to touch.

Before too long the tree was cleared,

The harvest all consumed;
The oranges had disappeared,
The muslin bags all strewn.

But Eric's heart had ceased to pound
And no one heard him sigh -
There weren't enough to go around;
He went to bed to cry.

He just could not believe his eyes
When at last he woke;
It took some time to realise
That it was not some joke.

A heap of muslin bags were there,
Arranged upon the bed;
Each one assembled with great care
And each one tied with thread.

As every bag he opened up,
He smiled and felt so rich,
For every child had offered up
At least one segment each.

Eric coughed and wished me well;
His tale had all been told.
And as the evening darkness fell,
I left him in the cold.

Now you might call me gullible
If I believed one word.
Though they might have been incredible,
I loved the words I'd heard.

I'm not sure if I trusted him,
But do I really care?
He earned the feast I got for him…
For that was only fair.

Sometimes, when I struggle with self-doubt, I remind myself what amazing creatures we are – each one of us makes about 35,000 conscious or semi-conscious decisions every day… But wait, what if they're all wrong?

Achilles Tendonitis

Will my Achilles ever heal?

I'm afflicted with tendonitis
And can't run around like before.
Please tell me I beg
How it got in my leg -
That must be a breach of the law?!

I thought it was better this morning
And went for a walk after ten.
The outcome was grave -
It didn't behave,
So I dragged it back home again.

It's been hanging around since Christmas
Can I please give it up for Lent?
If it won't disappear
Before Easter is here,
I'm thinking of charging it rent.

Holes in the Sky

There are holes in the sky
Where the rain comes through.
Yeah, it kinda bugs me
And I bet it bugs you!

And they never get fixed;
Nobody knows why,
But it makes us all mad,
If we cannot stay dry.

But I've got the answer -
I think it's appealing!
We'll do it the same way
As fixing a ceiling!

You'll think I'm just crazy,
As mad as a hatter -
I need PVA glue
And a great big ladder!

Tennis

I was playing at the tennis club,
My turn to serve came round,
The ball flew off my racket frame
And was never ever found.

Having done it just that once,
It seems I couldn't stop!
The balls got stuck up in the trees
And wouldn't ever drop.

They told me I should watch the ball,
Be sure to bend my knees.
But the balls just flew much higher
Into the waiting trees.

The balls themselves have had enough.
Some just scoff and sneer,
While others hide in piles of leaves,
Paralysed with fear.

The officials wrote to tell me:
"There's rules you must observe -
The balls must stay inside the fence
Every time you serve."

They want to stop my membership,
They say I've lost my touch -
They can't keep losing all the balls,
It costs them far too much.

I think I see their point of view -

I've become a menace.
Although the club's a lovely place,
It's ruined by my tennis!

I think I'll find an indoor court.
Yes, that's where I should play.
Without those trees to aim for,
I think I'll be okay!

Listening to the Stars

At times the whispers call to you,
Murmuring through the night,
Like thoughts upon a far-off shore,
Fast ebbing out of sight.

No qualm of conscience burdens them.
They mind not being heard,
For all their undertones dissolve
Like snowflakes undisturbed.

The fleeting breaths suggest once more
A multitude of souls,
Who vainly flee the hunter's spear,
Where Orion now patrols.

But these sighs are tough as diamonds,
Embroidered to evoke
Mythologies of ancient times,
Writ large on midnight's cloak.

Orion bestrides the inky sky,
Locked in a timeless chase,
Right at his heels his trusty dog,
Forever keeping pace.

Not wary of the hanging moon,
Not fleeting like the dew,
These constants of the inky sky
Are sure and tried and true.

When life seems so ephemeral,

Like shadows insecure,
It helps to know that, like the stars,
Great things do still endure.

Just a Bad Week

Sometimes your days are back to front.
You don't get any sleep -
You're yawning in the daylight hours,
At night you're counting sheep.

Some days come and stay too long
And will not go away.
They put their feet up on the couch,
As if they mean to stay.

The other days are cruel to you
And make your luck turn bad.
The week becomes a tale of woe,
The worst you've ever had.

They say that luck will even out,
No need to fret or fear,
For even if this stuff persists,
A new week's nearly here!

Pigeons of Discontent

There's danger out there in the garden,
So do something indoors instead!
If you risk going out in the open,
A pigeon may poop on your head!

Pigeons these days are a menace;
We have to take care when we drive.
Last week I lost a wing mirror
To a bird on the M25.

They're bent on world domination;
But don't get afraid or upset:
Look how they crash into windows -
I don't think they're ready just yet!

The Moth

A busy moth flutters,
Luminous against the night.
It seeks to flee the driving rain.
For a moment it's lost from sight,
But reappears, indoors,
In brisk encounter with the light.
Raps against it with muffled sound

And falls in a

spiral to the

ground

.

My Heart

I wore my heart upon my sleeve.
You could watch it dance and sing!

But often love is misperceived.
Often sorrow does it bring.

And now my pain has no reprieve.
Now my heart is in a sling.

My Cousin is a Fungi

According to the phylogenetic tree, animals are heterotrophs and therefore closely related to slime moulds and mushrooms and toadstools. We share about 30 percent of our DNA with fungi, far more than we share with plants!

Well, how can it possibly be,
In the phylogenetic tree,
That mushrooms and mould
(Or so I've been told)
Are closely related to me?

What if hell actually freezes over one day? It would be pretty scary. At that moment, all those things that couldn't happen would suddenly happen.

Never Met Anyone as Smart as You

An ode to someone who passed a big exam.

Beats me how you get all that stuff in your head,
From early morning till it's time for bed.
Others may try but they don't see it through.
Never met anyone as clever as you.

From the banks of Loch Lomond to Timbuktu,
The island of Zanzibar and Kathmandu,
You crush all your exams like a coke can too!
Never met anyone as clever as you.

I've heard about Goethe and Hippocrates,
Leonardo and Einstein and Socrates.
I can't understand all the hullabaloo -
Never met anyone as clever as you.

I think we should celebrate, don't you agree?
Let's have a party for just you and me!
Why am I included? I haven't a clue!
Never met anyone as clever as you.

But I have to tell you it's my fervent wish
That you don't get any smarter than this,
I so hope it never occurs to you
That soon you'll be just as smart as *me* too!

Nothing for Christmas

I got a friend of mine a gift.
I thought she might be glad.
I tied it with a bow so fine,
But, hey, she just went mad!

'No, no! No gifts!' she said to me.
'Please, please, just get me nothing.'
At first I didn't understand -
I thought she might be bluffing!

I went to town and found the store
And marvelled at the shapes -
All kinds of nothing piled up high,
Right past the blinds and drapes.

They wrapped it up, I took it home,
Wrote her name upon the tag.
I was worried that it might escape,
So I kept it in the bag.

A Christmas gift of nothing -
Could anything be duller?
Well, actually, I think it's cool -
Just hope she likes the colour!

The Speed of Dark

Welcome to my dark side!

You never did listen to those that would help.
You never could share the things that you felt.
You're all smoke and mirrors, you think we're just fools.
You're never around when reality calls.

You think you're a victim but I just don't care.
You let yourself go and no one knows where.
Don't look for pity, you're in the wrong place.
What good is a mirror if you don't show your face?

You say you feel trapped but you never get out.
We can all hear you, you don't have to shout.
I won't interfere and I won't intervene.
You've got more issues than Time Magazine.

You like to pose questions but why should I care?
I gave you the answers, you left them right there.
You never say sorry, you don't have the grace.
What good is a mirror if you don't show your face?

Are you waving or drowning? Nobody knows.
You're in a place where nobody goes.
Those sharks in the water are not out to play.
You could be saved but you're swimming away.

Sometimes you have to be cruel to be kind.
It tears at my heart to leave you behind.

You always said you just wanted some space.
What good is a mirror if you don't show your face?

There's no trust in your eyes, not even a trace.
You can't be a winner if you're not in the race.
They say that a flame needs only a spark,
But you disappear at the speed of dark.

The Blind Man from Oban

There was a blind man from Oban
Who frightened the folk in his clan -
Went fishing for lobster
Caught Nessie, the monster,
And brought the beast home for the pan!

Because It's There

Edmund Mallory is believed to have replied to the question "Why did you want to climb Mount Everest?" with the retort "Because it's there".

Why climb a dangerous mountain?
I raise my hands in despair.
It's simple they say,
I'll get it one day -
You climb it just 'cos it's *there*!

Why climb a flippin' great mountain
That's steep and cold and immense?
So what's at the top? -
A bloomin' great drop!
How does this make any sense?

People get lost on mountains,
Sometimes they never get found.
And those that survive
Look barely alive -
I bet they wish they'd gone *round*!

Behind Every Cloud

I don't usually have very profound thoughts, but sometimes I manage it. I think it would be useful if our profound thoughts were to rise up into the atmosphere and form special clouds - maybe orange and mauve stripey ones to differentiate them from ordinary rain ones. As they cool down, they would condense and fall down as written text that people could collect for future reference. I'd invent funnel-shaped hats and become rich.

If my thoughts left my head in a cloud,
People would stand and read them aloud,
They'd get soaked in the rain
With the words from my brain -
But some words would not be allowed!

Two Tickets

Whatever we had then I'm sure that we've lost.
It won't be no good if our paths ever cross.
Have you said goodbye to the memories we share?
Maybe you're bitter or maybe don't care.
I was in a train station last night in a dream
And I had two tickets to what might have been.

A cold wind was blowing and the sky was all black,
I stood on the platform and stared at the track.
The announcer said something and I turned away,
For the message gets clearer with each passing day -
Trains don't go backwards except when you dream
And you can't take a ride to what might have been.

The Early Bird and the Worm

The worm is caught by the early bird,
Or so my mother declared.
It's not good enough to be second or third -
Be early and quick and prepared!

Proverbs are generally useful,
As most of us would confirm.
But has anyone ever considered this
From the perspective of the worm?

Geminids

The source of the Geminid meteor shower is the asteroid 3200 Phaethon, now recognised as the second largest space rock to threaten our planet! It passes every year, peaking during the second week of December, trailing its cloud of debris. In 2093, it'll make one of its closest approaches and pass within just 3 million kilometres of the Earth! Can't wait!

It happens in December,
Each and every year.
Raining down quite rapidly,
The Geminids appear.

I go into the garden
To watch the meteor shower.
Streaks of light traverse the sky -
Fifty in one hour!

My feet are frozen solid,
So it isn't *all* good news.
I think next time I gaze at stars...
I'll need to wear my shoes!

Autumn

The promise of woodland walks, a crescendo of colour, conker fights, the low sun dappled through the trees, lots of cosy evenings snuggled up at home… Nah! I've tried, but I've never really liked autumn.

At the tips of naked branches,
Orange leaves hang in clusters,
Expecting to fall.
The bracken crunches in protest
At your intruding feet
And the chestnuts fall.
Day dissolves into hoary mists
Over woods of all colours.
A darkness will fall.

Forgive the miserly squirrel,
Forgive the birds that don't sing,
For Nature, embittered, grits her teeth
At Winter's warning call.

Okay, so…

If my attempts to be poetic
Turned out to be really pathetic,
I cannot be lying
When everything's dying -
I just don't find autumn aesthetic.

Feelings

Anxious, angry, happy, sad - emotions make us feel alive. You have to take the rough with the smooth. We're fundamentally social animals and some of our emotions are complex social ones. We don't just have personal feelings - we have ones that mesh with the feelings of other people. In a sense, you could say that emotions are what make us truly uniquely human. That and pickled eggs. Oh and the Hokey Cokey.

I'm really not myself today -
I think I've caught emotion.
There must be some way I can get
A cure-all kind of potion?

It may not be a sickness,
But I need to take control.
If it's something I signed up for,
I'd like to unenroll.

Since these feelings have arrived,
I'll try my best to rule them.
But what I really want to know
Is how to uninstall them.

I don't want "Awws" and sappy hugs.
I'll say a terse goodbye,
For now you must excuse me -
I think I'm going to cry.

Lack of Sleep 1

One baking hot December day,
Or it may have been in June,
I think it was in the morning
Or maybe the afternoon,
I went to bed and shut my eyes,
But being too tired to sleep,
I ran and ran around a field
And started to count the sheep.
I wrote the number in my book
Using invisible ink.
By now I'd built up quite a thirst,
But I didn't want to drink.
All this is understandable
For I hadn't slept a wink -
Perhaps my brain was all worn out
Or was I now too smart to think?

Lack of Sleep 2

Last night I couldn't get to sleep
And I tried to work out why.
I didn't have anxiety
And my throat was not too dry.

I lay in bed and listened hard,
But I heard no hoots or howls.
The fox must be on holiday
And they must be short of owls.

There must be something else to write,
But my brain has gone to sleep,
Though sadly all the rest of me
Is still counting those damn sheep!

Recently, I started pondering about humanity. I think I was on my third ponder, when it hit me. Of course! To understand humanity you have to consider the word itself. It's basically made up of two separate words - 'huma' and 'nity'. But what do they mean? No one knows. They don't even mean anything in Latin. And so there you have it - that's why humanity is such a mystery to everybody.

Happy Birthday To You

Can you name the song which is played or sung the most throughout the English-speaking world? Well, it's not "Auld Lang Syne" or "For He's A Jolly Good Fellow." According to the Guinness World Records, it's the song "Happy Birthday to You", composed by Mildred J. Hill in 1859. It was first published in 1893, with the lyrics written by her sister, Patty Smith Hill, as "Good Morning To All."

I'd sing happy birthday to you,
But it's not what you'd want me to do.
The words might be right,
Correct and polite,
But you'd get nicer sounds from a zoo!

Human Turbojet

A friend of mine was quite unwell,
Her tummy was upset.
She couldn't help but burp and belch -
A human turbojet.

She belched before the sun came up
And belched at sunset time,
She even belched on Sundays
When all the church bells chime.

One day I went to call on her
But couldn't find a soul.
I phoned the missing persons desk
And airport ground control.

The doctor told her: "Mrs Smith,
Be careful what you eat -
I recommend this chilli dish.
It's made of magic meat."

Well, the cure was quite successful,
For ev'ry time she spoke,
There was no belching any more -
Her words went up in smoke!

The Lie

So this is a harvest from a seed of doubt,
I guess I'm lucky that I found you out.
You'll feast no more on the fruit of lies.
I see you now through your sad disguise.

You say it's nothing, just a small mistake,
But one little lie is all that it takes.
It hurts real bad when you tell a lie,
But it hurts me more that my trust will die.

I may forget it but I don't know when,
For how can I ever trust you again?
I may forgive you but I don't know how,
For why should I ever believe you now?

Pembrokeshire

There's a Welsh saying relating to the weather in that part of the world: "If you can see the top of the mountain, it's about to rain. If you can't see the top of the mountain, it's already raining!"

If it turns out sunny on the Pembrokeshire coast,
I think you should write and complain -
When you spend all your money on waterproof boots,
It'd better flippin' well rain!

I'll Just Smile Because We Met

My regrets go sore and fester.
The painful words are those unsaid.
It's no good wishing things were better,
Now the tears have all been shed.

Times like these are like no others.
I'm just a farmer in the storm.
The darkest clouds loom high above me,
Beating down the unripe corn.

Thoughts of you shine in the night sky.
They can't help me find a way.
My memories are reaching for you,
But cannot bring you back today.

Sunset's come around too early,
But the stars do not forget.
And I won't cry because you're gone now,
I'll just smile because we met.

I like to swim in the mystery of life until I'm completely soaked, then I like to dry off in the warm glow of something perfectly obvious. You can't stay mysterious for too long. You get all pruned and wrinkly.

Are You a Martian?

Life on Earth began around 3.8 billion years ago, but it may not have originated on our planet. There is growing scientific support for a theory known as panspermia that suggests life first started elsewhere in space and was carried here by comets and meteorites. Scientists have discovered amino acids in meteorites that landed on the surface of the Earth. In Antarctica, for example, they have identified a meteorite that was definitely launched from Mars many millions of years ago. They know it's from Mars because its composition matches up with the composition of the Martian surface and it also contains bubbles of gas that correspond to the chemical and isotopic composition of gases in the Martian atmosphere.

How did life start on planets like ours?
Could it be microbes came from the stars?

For life's building blocks
Are found in old rocks
That appear to have travelled from Mars.

To be honest I don't have a clue
If the theory is actually true,
But if it's not lies,
I won't be surprised...
I've had my suspicions 'bout you!

My Exercise Regime

I'd like to be more healthy
I've put on too much weight
I think I'll do more exercise
I'll start by running late

Then when I've had my breakfast
Of sausages and eggs
I'll walk off disappointments
And pull some people's legs

I'll get into hot water
I'm really good at that
I'll fly right off the handle
Onto my yoga mat

I'll jump to some conclusions
I'm good at skipping chores
After lunch it's diddly-squats
I'll do them round at yours

Then I'll push my luck around
Up and down some hills
I'll be bending over backwards
And running up some bills

I'll dodge responsibility
As long as it don't hurt
Then I'll stretch the truth a bit
And maybe dig some dirt

I'll carry lots of grudges

Go skating on thin ice
And just in case that's not enough
Repeat the whole thing twice!

Reality, like life itself, is what you make it. Unfortunately, I can't make it at all today as I've got a dental appointment.

Hamish and the Scottish Antid-oat

Poor Hamish was contagious.
He had the Scottish flu.
His skin had turned to tartan,
His hair and toenails too!

"Noo jist haud on!" the doctor said,
"It's gaein be awright!
Jus' soak your skin in porridge
All day and overnight."

He duly smeared his face and hands,
His hair and toenails too.
By midnight he was so improved,
He felt like someone new.

But soon he grew suspicious -
He didn't know for sure
If porridge masked the problem
Or really was a cure.

The doctor reassured him:
"Aye, it's an antidote!
But if yon tartan reappears
You'll need a second coat."

Procrastination

They say that I procrastinate
But that's not strictly true.
I simply like to contemplate
What else I'd like to do.

In time the stuff will all get done,
Who cares about the date?
I've heard them say that good things come
To those prepared to wait!

There *is* a trick, I must admit,
And, if you will allow,
I'll tell you all about it...
But maybe not right now!

A Cliffhanger

I've always wanted to write a cliffhanger! Um,
sorry.

We searched for my Welsh Uncle Griff,
Who left my aunt after a tiff.
At the edge of Wales
Were his fingernails,
Still clinging to Llandudno Cliff.

Catharsis

We praise ourselves for being strong
And quell the pain we feel.
We think our sadness must be wrong
And forge our hearts of steel.

Some people do this really well,
The heart's ruled by the head.
The one's who do it best of all
Are people who are dead.

Emotions are a normal thing
And it's okay to cry.
Storing feelings in a bottle
Is bound to go awry.

I think it's best to open hearts
And let them have their say.
No one ever freed a pain
By locking it away.

Digging a Hole

Monday to Friday, I dig a hole.
Dig dig dig dig dig.
Saturdays and Sundays, I dig some more.
Dig dig dig dig dig.

Okay, probably not the most beautiful poem ever,
but you've got to admit…. it's deep.

Of course there's a god – when day breaks, someone always fixes it! Sorry. That started out as a really profound thought, but it was *so* deep, by the time I pulled it out, it had got all lumpy and squished.

Cyberchondria

Cyberchondria is the internet-induced phenomenon whereby people obsessively search the internet about their health anxieties.

It could be bovine spongiform
Or restless legs disease.
My symptoms differ from the norm -
It could be *both* of these.

It could be a bulbous iris
Or wobbly spinal cord.
But it can't be West Nile Virus -
I've never been abroad.

Could be white nose syndrome,
But, hey, I'm not a bat.
It's not a mutant chromosome
Or anything like that.

So, it seems self-diagnosis
Is quite a dodgy thing,
For I suppose it could be just...
A pimple on my chin?

Earth Aligned with Mars

A fragment of a rainbow
Is melting in my hand,
The ambient dark must soon give up
Its diamond grains of sand.

Everything is transient
And nothing's meant to last,
Everything's just flakes of snow
That come and go so fast.

Dizzy now, I tip my head
And drink the milk of stars
And wonder what it signifies
When Earth's aligned with Mars.

This is quite beyond my grasp,
Just things I can't control.
If I could only understand
And see inside your soul.

Is that your face I see up there
In constellations bright?
Will anything remain at all
When darkness turns to light?

Your fleeting image wavers
Upon the ice below,
So fragile and ephemeral...
And I must let you go.

I've noticed there's been a proliferation of cookery
on TV and I'm worried that it will cause cookery
on the streets. The last thing we need is innocent
pedestrians being whisked away by gangs of sous
chefs. I think TV glamourises cookery. And the
consequences of digesting food are rarely depicted.

The Shopaholic

A friend of mine went shopping once.
She didn't know what for,
But somehow she'd convinced herself
She needed one thing more.

She started on a Saturday
And went from store to store.
By Friday she was tired out -
Her feet were really sore.

She didn't know what she wanted;
Perhaps she never will.
Although the shops are boarded up,
They say she's out there still.

My Shoulder Blades are Missing!

I went to have physio following a shoulder injury. The therapist told me she was having a bit of trouble locating my shoulder blades!...

My shoulder blades are missing!
I don't know where they are.
They might be in the bathroom -
They can't have gone too far.

Did I have them yesterday?
I'm pretty sure I did.
The last time they went missing
They turned up in Madrid.

They've been on two safaris,
And cruised around the Med
And skied on the Matterhorn
And shopped in Maidenhead.

I'm never gonna find them,
I think that's understood.
I'll have to get replacements -
I think they're gone for good.

Where do you get new shoulders?
They must be strong and broad.
I'll get them in Ikea -
The best I can afford.

I don't want self-assembly,

I'd never get it right.
There'd be a piece left over
And I'd be up all night.

I'll try them out tomorrow
Or maybe Wednesday.
I'll act like I don't care at all -
Make sure they shrug okay.

I won't take any chances -
I'll use the strongest tape,
Nuts and bolts and superglue.
The new ones won't escape!

Remedies for Shoulder Pain

The pain in my shoulders defies all the odds.
Please stop them from hurting, I appeal to the gods!
I've treated them nice
And wrapped them in ice.
I've given them treatment and stretches and prods.

I've tried exercising and tried ev'ry drug,
Spent the morning in bed, all comfy and snug.
They said that I oughta
Drink lots of water,
But now I just hiccup whenever I shrug!

Until The Thaw

I know it's a pain for those who want to travel and conduct their business safely and securely, but I love it when it snows. I can gaze for ages at the big white flakes slowly succumbing to gravity and forming a vast comforting white blanket contrasting against the dark grey sky above. It evokes happy childhood memories that otherwise lie dormant. And, for a few short hours, all of life seems to enter a ghostly state of suspension.

Fleecy snowflakes kiss the canvas
With brush-strokes light and fine,
As soft as childhood memories,
Freed from the hands of time.

They're coating all the earth below
Like flour through a sieve,
Or like a throng of weary moths
With nothing more to give.

As robins refrain from singing,
And children gaze in awe,
Rekindled feelings, freed at last,
Can dance until the thaw.

Didn't You Get My Email?

*Never gonna give you up, Never gonna let you
down, Never gonna run around and desert you,
Never gonna make you cry, Never gonna say
goodbye, Never gonna tell a lie and hurt you, Never
gonna send a reply to your email though because
I'm kinda busy right now...*

I haven't forgotten 'bout you -
My emails are not getting through.
They've come to a halt;
It isn't my fault -
They're stuck on the M42!

The Wall of Doom

Using a tennis practice wall (or backboard) is one of the best possible ways to improve your game. Really?

Something lurks behind the trees,
Beneath the midnight moon.
It makes me feel so ill at ease -
The evil wall of doom.

By daylight, it seems harmless,
But do not be deceived.
It sneers at all your efforts
And makes you feel aggrieved.

By night, it seems to represent
The entrance to a tomb,
Where many wretched ghosts lament
And curse the wall of doom.

And though your best shots pepper it,
It won't let you improve.
Just when you think you've bettered it,
The white line seems to move.

You reenact your worst defeats;
You can't escape the gloom.
No one smiles for no one beats
The dreaded wall of doom.

Even the wall of Jericho
Was smashed and broken up.
Shall we send ours to Mexico

Addressed to Donald Trump?

No, maybe we should let it rot;
The mortar will crack soon.
And then we'll hit our hardest shots
And beat the wall of doom!

I'd follow my dreams, but I strongly suspect they don't know the way...

Oh wait, I can turn that into a poem:

A clock that don't work is right twice ev'ry day
But I'm always wrong whatever I say.
My luck has run out
I'm drowning in doubt.
I'd follow my dreams, but they don't know the way.

At Your Disposal

I ripped the knees of my best blue jeans
When I was just a kid.
I threw them out with the household trash -
Can't believe I did!
My mum just stood there sighing
With a needle and a thread.
I guess I never listened to a single word she said.

I met a girl - lived down the street -
And we became good friends.
We fought one night, I don't know why.
I told her it must end.
Well she just stood there crying
And her heart it must have bled.
I guess I never listened to a single word she said.

Now the boot is on the other foot
And you've walked out the door.
My heart knows there's another way.
It's irony for sure
That I've just stood here swearing
That our love cannot be dead
And you've refused to listen to a single word I've said.

Life Through the Rear View Mirror

My concept of time soon departed
When Gemma was learning to drive.
I didn't know when we'd get started,
I didn't know when we'd arrive.

Well I think what caused my confusion
Was all the time we spent in reverse.
It created a kind of illusion
Of a rear-facing universe.

There weren't any other big factors -
It's not like she drove very fast,
But hour after hour we went backwards
Like travelling into the past.

Car parks now send me all crazy
As I manoeuvre into a bay.
The clock on the dash goes all hazy
And I plunge into yesterday.

So it's really become a dilemma,
I'm puzzled and dazed and bemused,
Just thinking 'bout driving with Gemma
Has got me mixed up and confused.

Is this the start or end of the poem?
Did I somehow write in reverse?
Not sure if I'm coming or going...
You might have to read this bit first.

Food for Thought

One day it just happened to me -
I ate a thesaurus for tea!
I choked on a noun,
It wouldn't stay down -
An attack of hyperbole!

The long words would not go away;
I knew what the doctor would say -
"Don't grimace or frown;
You must swallow down
A spoonful of Tipp-Ex each day!"

Are we ever going to make any progress when our scientists are so clumsy? They've broken new ground, cracked the genetic code and split the atom.

Tuesdays

Nothing ever happens on Tuesdays,
So I have nothing to write.
I don't recommend that you read this;
Just do it to be polite?

Tuesdays aren't at the end of the week,
Nor are they right at the start;
They're not even bang in the middle -
It's like they're right off the chart.

A Tuesday would be so much better
If it would make up its mind,
And sneak in right next to a Thursday
Or leave the weekdays behind.

I think they're in need of a rescue
Or else they'll just fade away.
We could all agree to make Tuesday
National Bubble Bath Day.

We could act like penguins on Tuesdays
And hop and waddle and slide.
We could drink all our drinks with chopsticks
And wear pyjamas outside.

But the truth is, Tuesday's are boring,
They don't delight or enthral.
Weekends would come around quicker if....
We don't have Tuesdays at all!

Awesome Sports Accessories

I got a new grip for my racket.
It seemed like a sensible plan.
It cost me an absolute packet
And came all the way from Taiwan.
It fell off the first time I used it,
So I guess I'm not really a fan.

The next thing I got was a headband,
To keep the hair out of my face.
It was made by one of the top brands,
So I entered myself in a race,
But it slipped and I had to use both hands
Just to keep the damn thing in its place.

I got me a waterproof sports cap
So I wouldn't miss out on a game.
I got soaked the last time I used it -
The holes in it are really a shame.
You might ask me why did I wear it -
Well... I just didn't think it would rain!

Save the Vultures!

Poachers poison vultures because they circle above the carcasses of animals such as rhinos and elephants, revealing their location to rangers and wardens. Many species of vulture are now in danger of imminent extinction . I entered this poem in an International Vulture Awareness Day Literary Competition. Did it win? No.[*]

I'll get by with a little help from my friends.

Vultures are my favourite bird!
Now you might think I jest -
They don't have showy feathers,
Their bald heads don't impress.

They might seem fierce when you behold
That hooked and mighty beak,
But they don't catch their prey themselves -
Their feet are far too weak.

The vultures in The Jungle Book

Were based upon a band
That gave us fab pop music like
'I wanna hold your hand'.

But if you think that vultures sing,
You're in for quite a shock.
Grunting, hissing, barking sounds -
It's hardly classic rock.

You might just disagree with me -
I'm sure some people would.
But I believe they're special birds
That do a lot of good.

For a world without the vultures
Would be a smelly place.
And without these unsung heroes,
Disease would spread apace.

We shouldn't take objection to
Their rather grim cuisine.
Although it seems quite gross to us,
They keep things nice and clean.

In the struggle for survival
They're running out of luck.
I've heard that poachers poison them -
Well that just chokes me up.

When rangers hear of incidents,
Towards the scene they dash.
Response kits are the vital tools,
For which they want our cash.

The vultures need our help right now,
Or soon they won't be here,
So let's do what we can today
Before they disappear.

* *Actually, that's a lie. It won! And I've subsequently adopted a vulture at the Hawk Conservancy Trust in Andover..*

If you're going boating, it's probably a good idea to carry a swimming hat folded up in your pocket. If you fall in, you put on the hat while you're underwater and then come up to the surface, swimming all nonchalantly as if you meant to do it all along.

Big Mac and Fries

Valentine's Day and the card shops are closed;
I found some roses but they look decomposed.
You'll like this song, it's so subtle and deep.
It's got the words that will make your heart leap.
You won't want chocolates or a fine diamond ring.
You'll know my heart when I walk up and sing:

We're like Barbie and Ken, cow pats and flies,
Laurel and Hardy, Morecambe and Wise.
We fit together like a big mac and fries.

You're always saying that romance is dead,
Flowers forgotten and verses unread.
I wrote this song to show it ain't true.
I've found the words to describe me and you.
So we don't need Shelley and we don't need Keats.
I'll sing out loud in the roads and the streets:

We're like Barbie and Ken, cow pats and flies,
Laurel and Hardy, Morecambe and Wise.
We fit together like a big mac and fries.

A Cigarette

Had no sleep for days now,
He taps his bayonet.
Despite his shaking fingers,
He lights a cigarette.

Picks up the sound of wailing.
Old man staggers from a tent,
Turns red eyes to the soldier,
Breaks off his sad lament.

There's gunfire in the city.
Both seem to just forget.
Sat together by the roadside,
They share a cigarette.

Poetry and Inner Peace?

I thought poetry might be my way of cultivating inner peace… But how is that going to happen when those inner voices won't SIT DOWN AND SHUT UP?!

They say poetry is good for the soul?
- *What's good for the soul is some beans!*
What about the magic of metaphor?
- *I don't even know what that means!*

It may open doors to your feelings?
- *Nah, I think I'll keep those doors shut!*
It might help resolve inner turmoil?
- *Well, that makes you sound like a nut!*

Poems release all your hopes and your dreams?
- *I don't think they **should** be set free!*
But it teaches us cadence and rhythm?
- *It's no good. We'll never agree!*

Why Did the Chicken Cross the Road?

A chicken crossed the road one day
It wasn't clear what for.
Sometimes it's good to walk the way
You've never walked before.

Before she'd gotten very far
She wandered to the right.
She could have got to Potters Bar
Before the morning light.

Perhaps there was a roundabout,
Perhaps she took a fork,
Perhaps her little legs gave out
And just refused to walk.

There could have been a pothole there,
Or puddles oh so deep.
Perhaps she said a quiet prayer
And drifted off to sleep.

She might have tried some yoga too,
Went hopping with a frog?
She could have lit a barbecue
Or started up a blog.

The question's asked throughout the land:
Why did she go across?
The people want to understand.
They're wholly at a loss.

Perhaps inside she'd heard the call
That told her just to dare,
For sometimes surely don't we all
Get tired of standing there?

But it's so inconsequential,
Our logic's misapplied -
Is it always so essential
To reach the other side?

Nonsense

I thought you *liked* my nonsense,
I never thought to stop,
I thought you laughed your head off,
Ha ha ha ha ... plop!
But I was just deluded -
Your head was screwed on tight,
And if I can't do nonsense,
I don't know what to write!

The End

Now that you've come to the end of the book,
I hope that you didn't take too long a look.
I'm sorry, my friends,
I can't make amends -
You'll never get back the time that it took.

INDEX

A Cigarette 112

A Cliffhanger 85

Achilles Tendonitis 44

Andromeda.. 22

Are You a Martian? 78

At Your Disposal 101

Autumn.. 67

Awesome Sports Accessories 106

Basil 12

Beans on Toast... 27

Because It's There 62

Behind Every Cloud 63

Big Mac and Fries.. 111

Carrie's Magic Flask of Tea 18

Catharsis.. 86

Cyberchondria 89

Didn't You Get My Email? 97

Digging a Hole... 87

Earth Aligned with Mars 90

Eric and the Christmas Orange 40

Feelings 68

Food for Thought... 103

Geminids.. 66

Hamish and the Scottish Antid-oat.......................... 83

Happy Birthday To You 72

Holes in the Sky 45

Human Turbojet.. 73

I'll Just Smile Because We Met................................. 76

Just a Bad Week 51

Lack of Sleep 1 69

Lack of Sleep 2 70

Life Through the Rear View Mirror....................... 102

Listening to the Stars... 49

Minnows in a Stream... 16

My Cousin is a Fungi... 55

My Doomy Gloomy Universe 32

My Exercise Regime 80

My Heart 54

My Shoulder Blades are Missing! 93

Never Met Anyone as Smart as You 57

Nonsense 116

Nothing for Christmas 58

Pembrokeshire 75

Pigeons of Discontent 52

Poetry and Inner Peace? 113

Politics 17

Procrastination 84

Remedies for Shoulder Pain 95

Sand Creek 28

Sardines in a Can 35

Save the Vultures! 107

Snoring 24

Social Media and the Fruit Fly 6

Something I Wanted To Tell You 14

Tennis 47

That'll be Me... 26

The Blind Man from Oban 61

The Early Bird and the Worm 65

The End 117

The Headless Pigeon..................................... 34

The Lie... 74

The Martian 37

The Missing Moon 5

The Moth 53

The Olive Branch.. 36

The Shopaholic.. 92

The Speed of Dark.. 59

The Swallow 20

The Time Travel Paradox................................ 8

The Wall of Doom... 98

To Bee or not to Bee 15

To Boldly Go 11

Tuesdays 105

Two Tickets 64

Until The Thaw 96

We Shall Never Surrender 30

Why Did the Chicken Cross the Road? 114

Other books by David Winship

The Moon Pigeon, 2019, ISBN 978-1090321930

The Battle of Trafalgar Square, 2018, ISBN 978-1724086884

ANTimatter, 2018, ISBN 978-1986340724

ANTidote, 2016, ISBN 978-1530860722

Through The Wormhole, Literally, 2015, ISBN 978-1508718406

Stirring The Grass, 2016, ISBN 978-1492952725

Off The Frame, 2001, ISBN 978-1482793833

Talking Trousers and Other Stories, 2013, ISBN 978-1484898420

Printed in Great Britain
by Amazon

85419203R00072